For all the children of Aucors.
— C.M.

Many thanks to Vanesa Gutierrez, Lawrence Kim, E.Z., and T.Z.
for their precise and insightful contributions to the translation.
— C.Z.B.

www.enchantedlion.com

First American edition published in 2013 by Enchanted Lion Books, 20 Jay Street, M-18, Brooklyn, NY 11201
Translation Copyright © 2012 by Enchanted Lion Books
Translated by Claudia Zoe Bedrick
Originally published in France by Flammarion © 2011 as **Le Slip de Bain ou les pires vacances de ma vie**
All rights reserved under International and Pan-American Copyright Conventions
A CIP record is on file with the Library of Congress
ISBN: 978-1-59270-141-4
Printed in February 2013 in China by South China Printing Co. Ltd.

THE
BATHING
COSTUME

or

The Worst Vacation of My Life

By
Charlotte
Moundlic

Illustrated by
Olivier
Tallec

ENCHANTED LION BOOKS
NEW YORK

In a month, my family will be moving. So my parents have decided that this summer I'll go away kind of on my own, which means without Mama.

I'll go with my grandparents to their house in the country. As for my brother Martin, he's going to visit his penpal Steven in Southampton, England.

I've never had to go away without Mama before. Since she doesn't work, she always goes with us on vacations. Papa usually stays in Paris for work and joins us on the weekends, except, of course, when he's on vacation, too.

Papa told me about this last night and I could see that it really got to Mama. She didn't say anything, just wiped her eye gently, pretending like she had something in it. I wasn't very brave either, which makes sense, since I'm not used to being without her.

Martin burst out laughing, super happy to have something to tease me about. "So, Bonnie Ronnie, you're going to have to go away without dear Mama?"

He annoys me so much! So I kicked him, to make him punch me back. This way I could cry as much as I wanted while he got punished.

My name is Myron and I'm almost eight years old. Having such an old-fashioned name isn't always fun, believe me. It's all Grandpa Myron's fault. He was my father's father, and he died right before I was born. Since Mama was sure she'd have a girl—thanks to Aunt Nadine, who's never wrong—she unthinkingly agreed to the name to make Papa happy. Then, when I was born, it was too late to take it back.

To give me a cuter name, Mama nicknamed me "Ronnie," which Martin quickly changed to "Bonnie Ronnie." He's twelve and hates me. But guess what? I hate him even more.

I leave on Friday for a week.

Day One

When we arrived at the front door we could barely see the house because there were so many overgrown plants everywhere. But with us there, I felt the house would begin to come out of its long hibernation. Grandpa said the plants would give us some real work to do, but I don't really want to garden with him because he scares me a little. He doesn't talk much, so you never know what he's thinking. Also, he's usually pretty strict.

Even more than Mama's absence, the bad news of the summer is that the cousins are also coming. Jean, Edgar, and Hector, the three sons of Uncle Patrick, Mama's older brother. It's bad news because they're big, strong, and buddies with Martin. I'm the butt of all their jokes.

Grandma asked me if I was happy and I muttered, "Yes... Yeah, sure..." What else could I say? I didn't want to tell her that I was about to have the worst vacation of my whole life.

Grandma also told me that at my parents' request she's going to have me do a little work every day. After summer vacation, I'll be going into third grade. I'm the shortest in my class and I haven't lost a single tooth. To top it all off, my teacher noticed that I've been having some difficulties with writing. On my report card, in the comments section, she wrote: "A dreamy, distracted student who is very nice to all of his classmates."

Grandma explained that since they don't have a telephone, she's going to have me write Mama a letter. I'll write a little bit every day. That way I'll have something to send her at the end of the week. I asked if I could start tomorrow, since except for throwing up during the car ride, I don't have anything to tell.

Grandma agreed with a smile.

Day Two

Right now, I'm nibbling on the end of my pencil. I have no idea what to write. If I tell Mama that just after arriving Jean and Edgar short-sheeted my bed, she'll come get me immediately and I'll seem like even more of a baby.

But then, just like that, I start:

Dear Mama, I hope you're doing well.
It's beautiful here...

That will be it for today. I prefer not to think too much about her since it makes me a little sad. I'll see what tomorrow's like.

Day Three

If I were to be completely honest, I'd tell Mama that I was the one who suggested to the cousins that we hold a competition to see who can wash the least over the vacation. I came up with this plan because the bathroom is really, really old and the shower is full of spiders.

When Grandma tells us to go wash up, we head for the bathroom, where we draw straws to see which of us has to stay. The loser has to shower for real, while the rest of us make noise so it seems like we've all gone in.

Anyway, we're not really that dirty. Plus there's only enough hot water for one shower. But since Mama thinks being clean is really important, I didn't say anything in the letter. Otherwise Grandma would get in trouble and that wouldn't be fair. So all I put was:

I'm having a good time. Tomorrow we'll go biking.
I'm eating everything Grandma serves,
including the green vegetables. ~~Even seconds~~.

I wrote that to make her happy.

But then I crossed out the stuff about seconds because there's no way she'd ever believe me...

Day Four

Today we went biking. Without helmets.

It was amazing.

Normally, I'm not allowed to even get on my bike without a helmet. But my cousins said that I could do whatever I wanted since Mama isn't here. Ever since I had that idea about the shower they've been a lot nicer. So I said "'K," to sound cool.

Then they showed me this really great thing where you can make your bike sound exactly like a motorcycle by attaching a playing card between the spokes with a clothespin. Suddenly you're zooming and you're king of the road.

After that, Hector suggested that we steal some logs and planks from the woodhouse to make ramps. Usually we're not allowed to go there because that's where Grandpa keeps his tools and the chainsaw. So I was put on lookout. None of us got caught.

We made a stunt course all along the path by balancing the planks on the logs.

We laughed so hard!

At the start I had the jitters, but with our motors and the ramps it was like we were motorcycle racing. We did these really crazy jumps, too!

All I added today to my letter was:

This afternoon we did some great biking!
We're going to go to sleep early. I think I have a loose tooth.

My parents are really busy with the move, so it's not worth worrying them for nothing. Also, my tooth really is loose. I'm so happy!

Day Five

Today we went to the swimming pool.
Normally, I really like going, but today it was
a nightmare...

This summer I'm eight. And in the family,
the summer when you're eight is the summer when
you have to jump off the 10-foot diving board.

At first I thought that I'd be able to escape the whole
thing thanks to Grandpa's old car, which spent the winter
here and wouldn't start. Since there were six of us, we
were too many for Grandma's car. But Grandpa said it would
be okay to put two of us in the back of Grandma's car since
the pool is nearby. This time he was the one who said it would
be best not to mention anything to Mama.

"Boys, don't forget your bathing costumes!" Grandma called.

Hearing her call our swimsuits that really cracked me up.

I sat in the back with Jean. As we drove, I suddenly realized that I could dive off the 3-foot diving board today and save the high board for the last day since we'd be going back to the pool at the end of the week. That way I'd gain time.

I really have no idea how I'm going to do this because I'm so terrified of the high board. Before I left, Mama told me that she'd prefer if I jumped on a day when she was there. But if I don't do it now I'll be so ashamed that I'll never be able to come back here again. Not next year or any year after that.

When we got to the changing room, I put on my suit. Well, no, not mine exactly. Martin's, which is way too big for me. Suddenly the swimming pool was transformed into my worst nightmare. I had to hold on to my suit the entire time because everyone kept trying to pull it off.

I tried the low board and, as I had feared, I found myself in the water with my bottom in the air. That really gave the cousins something to tease me about. All I wanted to do was cry, so I bit the insides of my cheeks to stop myself.

In the car on the way back, Grandma said that she would sew something into my suit so it would stay up next time. Hector said, "Why not suspenders?" This made everyone roar, even Grandpa. I don't ever want to go back there again.

I didn't add anything to my letter today, mostly because I'm mad at Mama. Since Grandma saw that I was sulking, she didn't insist.

Day Six

Last night was the scariest night of my life! Suddenly the sky burst open and lightning flashed through the dark clouds. Then, the lights went out. We were just going into our room when Grandpa came to get us, carrying a lit candle. He gave each of us our own candle and suggested we stay with him and Grandma in the living room while we waited for things to calm down. I was glad because for once not even the big cousins acted brave. We went downstairs single file to where Grandma had made a fire in the old fireplace.

Grandpa told us stories about when he was a kid. He used to come to this same house with his five brothers and his cousins. They did tons of hilarious things together. It was funny because it all sounded just like me and my cousins, except that back then they went swimming in the river since the city pool didn't exist yet.

Then Grandma made us hot chocolate and the lights came back on.

When we got back to our room, we fell asleep right away without telling any jokes.

Before closing my eyes I thought that I should write this to Mama: "Grandma takes really good care of us, and I'm not scared of Grandpa anymore."

It's true. Since realizing that he used to be a kid, too, I'm not frightened of him anymore.

Day Seven

So, this is it. We're leaving tomorrow. The vacation has whizzed by, and, I have to admit, I've had a super good time. But before I can declare victory, I still have to face the hardest test of my life. To be honest, I still don't know how I'm going to do it. If I survive, I'll gladly sacrifice myself to the shower tonight.

It's time to leave for the pool, so I dawdle a little, hoping they'll forget me. But I know I'm just dreaming, because my 10-foot jump is definitely something they're all waiting for.

I hear Grandma calling: "Ronnie, let's go!"

So, I go...

Grandma has sewn a horrible elastic thing into my bathing suit to hold it up. But since she's not good at sewing, my suit now looks like a diaper. And I look like a sissy. Everyone in the locker room snickers at me.

To get it over with, I'm going to begin with the jump. I concentrate as hard as I can as I walk toward the diving board. I drag my feet as I reach the ladder. The main thing is not to look up. I begin to climb, but my legs tremble and big drops of sweat pour down my forehead.

They're all there. Grandma and Grandpa to the right of the ladder. Jean, Edgar and Hector to the left. I hear them egging me on.

From one side, they shout: "Ronnie, you're a champion!"

From the other: "Bonnie Ronnie is a chicken!"

I block out their voices so I won't lose my focus.
I climb and climb and climb. It seems like I'll never stop.
Then... I'm there. It only took a few seconds but it felt like hours.

The diving board seems to go on forever. I try not to look down.
I check that my bathing suit is still in place, but I accidentally pull
at a thread and the elastic that Grandma put in comes out with it.

Now I'm really done for. But since I'm already here, there's no way
I can turn back.

Just as I'm about to jump to my death, I feel something warm in my mouth. I lick the inside of my cheek. Yup, it's blood. Pressing down with my tongue, I feel that my tooth is about to fall out. I try to get it with my finger, but I press too hard and it pops right out of my mouth.

Oh, no! My tooth!

I shout: "My tooth! My tooth has fallen into the water. We have to find it!"

Then I see Jean, followed by Edgar and Hector, jump into the pool to look for it.

This is my lucky break, since I really don't want them to witness my disastrous dive. The important thing is to be really careful and not collide with them.

I have only a few seconds, so I jump, and before I know it I'm flying through the air and hitting the water at full speed.

I try to hold up my bathing suit, which has slipped down, but I really can't be bothered. Thanks to my tooth, I did it! And no one saw my bottom, except my grandparents. Grandma nudges Grandpa, who winks at me and claps like a madman.

Hector climbs out of the pool holding my tooth between his thumb and index finger. We've done it! And I think I can say for sure that this has been the best day of my whole life by far!

Mama, of course, will have to buy Martin a new bathing suit. Grandma's stitches are now completely messed up and I've pulled the waist out so far that it's now Papa who can wear it.

I'm really sad to be leaving tomorrow. This afternoon, Grandpa took us to the river where he swam as a kid. We decided to have a picnic dinner there, and to celebrate my feat, we sang. I feel like the cousins respect me now.

I'll be going to sleep soon. I asked Grandma if we could forget about sending Mama the letter. She agreed. I still reread it before throwing it out. It was completely worthless, so I crumpled it up. The only thing I'd like to write to Mama is: I want to have exactly the same vacation next year.

Well... almost... Only with a "bathing costume" that fits.